PUFFIN BOOKS

RAT SATURDAY

When Joe plucks up the courage to pay a visit to old Mr Tetley, rumoured to have a cellar full of rats, he finds himself being introduced to Rodney and Wilfred, two very friendly, very tame pet rats. Joe and his lively friend Donna are soon visiting 'Old Teabag' every day, and they discover that pet rats can be a lot of fun.

Margaret Nash is a former children's librarian in Luton and South Hertfordshire. She keeps pet rats herself and belongs to the National Fancy Rat Society. *Rat Saturday* is her first book.

MARGARET NASH

RAT SATURDAY

ILLUSTRATED BY MAGGIE LING

PUFFIN BOOKS

For Clive, Adrian and Paul, with Love

Puffin Books, Penguin Books Ltd, Harmondsworth, Middlesex, England
Viking Penguin Inc., 40 West 23rd Street, New York, New York 10010, U.S.A.
Penguin Books Australia Ltd, Ringwood, Victoria, Australia
Penguin Books Canada Limited, 2801 John Street, Markham, Ontario, Canada L3R 1B4
Penguin Books (N.Z.) Ltd, 182–190 Wairau Road, Auckland 10, New Zealand

First published by Viking Kestrel 1984
Published in Puffin Books 1986

Made and printed in Great Britain by
Richard Clay (The Chaucer Press) Ltd,
Bungay, Suffolk
Typeset in Monophoto Palatino

Chapter One

Joe tinkled the busfare money in his trouser pocket. Yes, he would spend it on Jawbreakers, which would last all the way home. Thank goodness he wouldn't see Dobbie Wilson and Jason Tucker in the shop. They were going on the bus, which was why he was walking. Joe's cheeks went red as he remembered that dreadful game of football. Mr Slater had made him goalie and Joe had dreaded the ball coming near. Suddenly there it was, hurtling towards him, but as it came nearer Joe had run out of the goalposts and let them score. Mr Slater had yelled. Some boys had laughed at him and Jason's team had cheered. Joe had felt very silly. He still felt silly.

The sweet shop was crowded. Old Teabag was at the front of the queue counting out his money on the glass counter. Joe hadn't seen the old man for a while. He was nicknamed 'Teabag' because his real name was Tetley, like the teabags. There were various stories going round at school about Old Teabag. Someone said he lived in a cellar with rats, and shared his food with them. Penny Lawson, who lived opposite him in Summer Street, said he sat by a lamp and wrote on large sheets of paper all through the night. She said he was a spy.

When Joe came out of the shop Teabag was bending down picking up chocolate drops from a burst sweet bag. Joe began to help the old man. Some of the chocolate drops rolled into the gutter. Teabag picked them up too! Joe watched in amazement.

He'd often stuck his chewing-gum on the canal bridge while fishing but even he wouldn't eat chocolate drops out of the gutter. Teabag seemed to know what Joe was thinking.

'Oh, they're not for me,' he explained, 'they're a treat for the rats!'

Joe's Jawbreaker suddenly felt so large in his mouth he thought it might really break his jaw. He whisked it out of his mouth into his hanky. It must be true then; Teabag did live in a cellar with rats. He started to walk quickly, but Old Teabag kept up with him.

'Had a good game of football?' asked the old man, looking at the bulging cloth bag.

Joe's stomach twitched unpleasantly. 'No,' he answered, 'I'm not much good at games.'

'How about homework?' joked Teabag.

'We don't get much in the 9 + ,' said Joe.

Teabag changed the subject again.

'Have you any pets waiting for you at home?'

'I wish I had,' said Joe. 'Mum says they make work.'

'Aye, they do, lad, but they're nice to have around.' They were nearly at the corner of Summer Street now. 'Pop in and see my animals sometime; I live at number three.' He winked, and with a friendly wave Thomas Tetley turned left into Summer Street.

Joe ran the rest of the way home. As he

swung into Chiltern Way he took the heavy hanky from his pocket and started to unpleat it. He bunged the messy ball back into his mouth. Better to have his mouth full and then he couldn't answer Mum when she asked if he'd had a good day; if he'd played football and why he'd missed the bus.

There was a tasty smell of baking in the kitchen. On the work-top stood jam tarts in gleaming red lines like polished soldiers.

'For the church bazaar,' said Mum, as Joe eyed them. She let him eat one all the same. She slid fish-fingers under the grill and Joe put two knives, two forks and two plates on the table.

'I met Old Teabag; you know, the man who sometimes rides that big three-wheeled bike,' he said.

'Oh, you mean Mr Tetley. He's a nice old man.'

'Teabag said I could go and see his pets

sometime,' said Joe. 'Don't think I will
though,' he added. He sighed. 'Oh Mum, I
do wish you'd let me have a dog or cat or
something.'

'Now don't start all that again, Joe,'
snapped his mother. 'You know we've no
room for one.'

Joe didn't know. He knew it was an
excuse, and that she just didn't want one. He

pushed his plate to one side, helped himself to another tart and went into the lounge. He turned the television on loud and curled up in one of the big chairs to watch what was left of the children's programmes.

Chapter Two

Joe woke up with his 'let's do something exciting' feeling. Then he remembered the church bazaar. Ugh! He didn't want to get involved with that. The church ladies always treated him as though he were still six years old and Mum kept saying, 'Oh Joe will do that, won't you Joe?' in a special sing-songy voice. He'd go fishing — by the canal — that's what. It was like a different world down there; peaceful and interesting.

After breakfast Joe got his gear ready. Mum wasn't too keen on the idea and kept fussing. In the end Dad told her to stop it.

'Leave the lad alone, Jan,' he said, 'you'll make him into a softy.'

Joe felt a tinge of pride as he always did when Dad stuck up for him. Besides, Dad liked him to do sporty things.

Soon Joe was sitting by the gentle canal. It was a while since he'd been. The water-level had risen a few inches; that was good. The canal looked happier when it was full.

'Hi!' said a voice suddenly, 'caught anything?'

Joe looked up to see a ginger-haired girl. It was Donna Spinks, who was in his class at school. Joe felt a scowl coming on and muttered, 'No, not yet.' He hoped she would go away. She started kicking an old Coke tin around.

'Don't do that,' he said, 'you'll scare the fish.' Donna stopped and sat down beside him. She swung her legs against the canal

13

bank and rocked from side to side, humming
a stupid tune.

'Bet you've never caught anything,' she
taunted.

'Course I have,' said Joe.

'Our Steve's good at fishing,' said Donna.
'He does it properly: you need a float. I don't
think you're doing it properly.' Joe shuffled
about on the uneven bank.

14

'Well go and watch him then, boss-cat!'

But Donna didn't. She stayed all morning. Jason Tucker passed along the towpath on his bike and did a silly whistle when he saw them together. Joe squirmed and felt annoyed with Donna.

'I'm off,' he said, gathering up his tackle.

'Me too,' persisted Donna. 'I'm hungry.'

As they trudged in silence towards the

park, Teabag passed, wobbling along on his trike. The wire basket was full of food. Joe waved and the old man waved back.

'Fancy waving to him,' said Donna. 'He's a queer old man.'

'It's all those rats he lives with,' said Joe. 'That's what all that food's for – to feed them with.' Donna was suddenly alert.

'Do you think it's true – those rats, I mean?'

'Yes,' said Joe.

'But Penny Lawson says he's a spy and she should know,' said Donna.

Joe didn't really see that Penny Lawson should know. He remembered Penny once telling the class that Miss Winterbottom had died at the weekend. Old 'Frozen Bum', as they called her, had walked in ten minutes later. Her car had broken down, that was all.

'Well, I know it's true,' said Joe.

'Go on,' said Donna, 'how?'

He told her about his talk with Teabag. He told her about the chocolate drops for the rats. Her eyes opened wide.

They spent the next few minutes trying to picture Old Teabag sitting in a damp cellar with rats running up his trouser legs.

'Do you think they squeak and squeal?' she said.

'Or gnaw and bite?' added Joe.

'I wonder how many there are.'

'I could go and see him,' suggested Joe. 'Teabag asked me to.' Donna looked at him, funny-like.

'Why don't you, then?'

Joe wrinkled his nose and sniffed. He wished he'd not said anything.

They were at the huge park gates already. Donna started to climb up one. Joe stared at her. He had always wanted to climb those tall gates but had never dared. She was already half-way up. He remembered Dad's words – 'You'll make a softy out of him.' He remembered the football lesson. He was a bit soft sometimes, he knew. The iron gate started creaking. Donna was hanging on with one arm and leaning out trying to make the big gate move.

'Go on, Joe,' she said, 'I dare you to go to Teabag's.'

'Right!' said Joe, suddenly feeling brave. 'Right, I jolly well will go and find out!'

He had a quick look round to see if anyone was watching, then said, 'Shove over, Donna, I'm coming up the gate.'

Chapter Three

Monday morning went slowly at school. Miss Winterbottom gave them all a spelling test. Buggy Donlan cheated and she went on and on about truthfulness.

As they went into 'musical expression', Donna passed him a note. Joe couldn't open it at once because he had to be a crab to some silly rippling sea music. But later he managed to read it.

'GO TONIGHT AFTER SCHOOL' it read. There was a funny little drawing of a rat. I will go, thought Joe. I'll go instead of staying on for stamp club, and he felt pleased with himself.

School dinner on Monday was always
yukky watery fish and dry potatoes. Today
the potato domes were so stiff you could
tunnel through without them collapsing.
Sammy Jeans, who sat next to Joe, did
windows and doors in his. They giggled
helplessly till Miss Winterbottom came over.

Afterwards Joe saw Donna in the
playground and wondered if he dared go
over to her. It was somehow different back at

school. He felt shy. She was with four other girls. Donna never mentioned the note.

However, at the end of school she was hanging around the gates. She started to skip alongside him in an irritating sort of way.

'Are you going?' she asked. Joe nodded. Donna stopped skipping. 'Right,' she said. 'I'm going to wait at the top of the street till you come out.'

Joe turned the corner into Summer Street and left Donna idly swinging round the lamp-post. He wondered what she would do while he was at Teabag's, but Donna Spinks was never one to be still for long, and as he reached the gate of number three she was already into a game of hopscotch.

Joe walked up the diamond-patterned path to the front door. The houses in this road were very tall and all joined together in blocks. He heard Old Teabag's wheezy cough just before the door opened. It took a

second for the old man to recognize Joe, but then he smiled and looked pleased.

'Hello, lad. Come in.' Joe stepped into the dim hall and Teabag opened another door for Joe to go through. They went into a large square room. There were clocks ticking everywhere. They sounded as though they were bickering among themselves. In the corner by the fireplace was a large writing-desk covered with clock springs, gears and bits and pieces. Joe knew it was rude to stare but he just couldn't help it.

'Sit down,' said Teabag, kindly.

Joe sat in a large squashy chair and kept looking round. Then his eyes fixed on something; something with a brown head and white body; something with a long thin tail. The something was sitting on the back of an old leather settee. Teabag picked it up and took it to Joe. 'Meet Rodney,' he said gently. Joe backed away a bit. The rat pushed its face forward and sniffed at Joe, its whiskers twitching all the time. It had shiny black eyes and delicate pink ears. Suddenly it turned back and ran up Teabag's arm. It sat on his shoulder and washed its paws hurriedly.

'Just a minute,' said Teabag. He bent down under the clock desk, grovelled around a bit and came up holding another rat, this time white.

'Meet Wilfred,' he said. Wilfred also did the sniffing trick, then slid down Teabag's leg and ran back to the corner where he'd been busy eating something. Joe wondered how many more there were. He had to know.

'Do you have more in the cellar?' he stuttered.

'Good gracious, no!' said Teabag, surprised. 'No, these are my pets! I've just the two of them and they live up here in that cage.' He pointed to a large cupboard-like object near the desk. 'Dick Bailey, my student lodger, lives in the basement, or cellar as you call it. He's got a cosy little bed-sit down there.'

Joe could have kicked himself. He'd almost believed silly Penny Lawson. The outlined figure by the lighted window was a lodger.

He sat back. Teabag brought Rodney over
to him.

'Stroke him,' said Teabag. Joe nodded.
'Now you stay with ... what's your name,
laddie?'

'Joe,' said Joe, 'Joe Sprattley.'

'You stay with Joe a minute.'

Teabag went out of the room then came
back with two glasses of milk and digestive
biscuits balanced on a large book. He gave

one glass to Joe. Rodney calmly helped himself to a whole biscuit and crumbled most of it on Joe's knee before running up and sitting on his shoulder.

'Do you mend clocks?' asked Joe looking around again.

'Aye,' said Teabag. 'Does all the ticking annoy you?'

'No, it's friendly,' said Joe. 'I like it.'

'Well, they've fascinated me all my life, Joe. I've been up and down the country learning about them. Have a look at some if you like.'

Quite a few of the clocks said three o'clock.

'I set all clocks that aren't working at three,' explained Teabag. 'That way I can tell at a glance which need repairing.'

Just then the clock by the window struck five. Others quickly joined in. Rodney shot down Joe's back and across the floor to his cage. He was inside it in an instant.

'That's my boy,' said Teabag, 'time to go back.'

'It's time I was going too,' said Joe.

'Do come again, lad. I like young company.'

'Can I bring a friend?' asked Joe.

'Of course!' said the old man, kindly, 'you do that.'

Joe ran up to the corner of Summer Street but Donna wasn't there. The road was empty. She must have gone home. No wonder, thought Joe. He'd been a long time. Thank goodness Mum would think he'd be at stamp club, or she'd be cross.

Chapter Four

Joe was almost at school next morning when Donna pounced.

'I waited ages last night, what happened?'

He told her excitedly about the rats.

'Only two rats?'

'Oh, but you should have seen them, they're lovely. I've asked Teabag if you can look at them sometime. The room is full of clocks too – clocks and rats.' Donna looked interested; she was always keen on a new venture.

Assembly took a long time that morning. The school had won a series of inter-school football matches. Mr Priggen, the head teacher, presented a silver cup to Jason Tucker. Jason was captain of the school team. Joe sighed. If only he were good at football. Of all the things to be good at, football seemed to be the best. Of course, he flung himself about on the pitch and got his clothes filthy so it looked good, but Joe rarely got near the ball. He just took home very dirty clothes which had to be soaked for days in a bright orange bucket. If only there was something he could get a cup for. Joe came back to reality when Miss Winterbottom prodded him to lead his line back to the classroom.

At playtime Donna spread the rat story. Soon everyone was pushing and shoving round him. 'Do they bite?' 'Are they smelly?' 'Is Teabag a spy?'

'No,' answered Joe, 'they're pets.'

Penny Lawson stuck her tongue out at him and said she didn't believe it, but no one took any notice of her. Then Buggy Donlan crashed in on the circle.

'Ugh,' he sneered, 'you can't have rats as pets, they spring at your throat.' He made a

sudden grab at Joe's neck and screeched. He turned to his two loyal followers, Dominic Stone and Leslie Tate. 'Ain't that right, lads?'

'Yeah,' they agreed. One or two of the

crowd looked uncertain now and shuffled away from Joe.

'Tame rats are different!' protested Joe.

'No, they ain't,' pouted Penny Lawson. 'I'm on your side, Buggy.'

Miss Winterbottom came striding towards them. Teachers never liked a crowd. They always suspected foul play. The children scattered. Donna came up with Sally Stephens tugging at her sleeve like a bramble.

'When shall we go and see the rats, Joe? Saturday morning?'

'OK,' said Joe.

'... call for you at ten, right?'

Saturday was a long way off to Joe. He had to see the rats again before then. If he ran most of the way home he could surely grab five minutes to whizz down Summer Street?

Teabag came to the door wearing Rodney

on his shoulder. The rat looked down at Joe, who was so out of breath he could hardly speak.

'Is it all right if Donna and I come round about ten thirty on Saturday, please?' he puffed.

''Course it is, lad.' Wilfred was curled up in one of the fireside chairs. Teabag gave him gently to Joe. He felt heavy and floppy as he settled down sleepily in Joe's lap. He looked

closely at the little heaving body, at the delicate fingers and toes, the pretty face. These little creatures so fascinated him. They were perfect in every way. He talked to Wilfred and the animal seemed to accept his words, with an occasional ripple of its fur as he stroked it.

Joe timed the five minutes on his watch. 'I must go now,' he said.

Teabag smiled. 'Call tomorrow; call any time,' he said.

Joe did. He called every single day before Saturday. Sometimes the rats were curled up cosily in their cage. Sometimes they were on the book shelves like a couple of book-ends. It became quite a game – 'Spot the Rat'.

Dad was scraping up the last of the dead leaves in the pale spring sunshine when Donna arrived on Saturday, but he broke off to say hello to her properly.

Mum gave them a couple of apples to eat. 'Your mum and dad are nice,' mumbled Donna, as they walked along the road, munching. Joe felt pleased.

They were soon at number three Summer Street. Joe opened the creaking iron gate of Teabag's tiny front garden, then stopped abruptly and stared. Leaning against the rickety fence was the twisted frame of Teabag's tricycle. The front wheel was badly buckled and the wire basket mashed up around the handlebars. A cold, sickly feeling punched Joe's stomach. Slowly he knocked at the door. Donna shuffled uneasily. He knocked again and waited, hoping to hear the old man's cough and slow footsteps, but there were neither.

'He'd be in,' said Joe, emptily. 'He knew we were coming.' There was nothing to do but go away. Just as they turned, a young man wearing a black leather jacket came hurrying towards them. He lifted his crash helmet and ran his fingers through his hair.

'We've come to see Mr Tetley,' explained Joe.

'The old boy's in hospital; ran his trike up a lamp-post.' Joe looked at the screwed-up trike again and didn't know what to say.

'... could 'ave been worse,' went on the youth, 'but the ambulance had to come. By

the way, I'm Dick Bailey, his lodger. I've just come back for some of his things to take to the hospital.'

'We came to see the rats,' said Donna, bluntly. 'Who'll look after them now?'

'I suppose I'll have to,' said Dick Bailey.

'We can do it,' offered Joe. 'Tea ... er, Mr Tetley, showed me how.'

'Fine by me,' replied Dick Bailey. 'If you come in the early evenings, then I can let you in.' Joe felt calmer inside. Look after the rats — that would be lovely and somehow he knew Teabag would approve. Dick Bailey showed them in and stood jingling his bike keys while Joe quickly showed the rats to Donna.

'I'll tell the old man you're going to look after them,' said Dick Bailey as he pressed his foot down strongly on the bike pedal. 'He'll be glad. He's very fond of those bloomin' rats.'

Chapter Five

Dick sped off in a blue haze of motorbike fumes, leaving them standing there.

'I hope Teabag will be all right. That trike looks horrible,' muttered Joe, staring at the ground.

'Yes,' said Donna, 'he must have hurt himself.' She looked miserable. There didn't seem anything interesting to do now and there was a whole empty day stretching ahead. 'I suppose we could go to our house,' she suggested. Joe slurred his toe idly in the earth.

'OK,' he said, but he didn't move. Donna shook his shoulder.

'Well, don't come if you don't want to; go home, I don't care.'

'All right, I'll come,' he said. She livened up and started twirling along in front of him.

'I know, let's play "last tap".' She tapped him smartly on the arm and ran off. Joe chased her but Donna slithered down to the ground in front of the postbox.

'You can't be tapped if you're sitting down!' she grinned. Fortunately for Joe, the postman appeared to collect the lunch-time post and she had to move.

They arrived at Donna's exhausted. Her mum was doing the washing. She looked hot and flustered, having just discovered a shredded tissue in the wash. She was shaking Donna's school blouse and bits of pink were floating everywhere. Some landed in her frizzy hair-do.

'Give us a hand, Donna,' she said, rolling

up her baggy sleeves. Donna looked as though she often gave a hand as she shook and folded the clothes.

'I know, why don't we go to the library this afternoon and see if they've got a book on rats?' said Donna. 'We ought to know all we can about them.'

'Good idea,' agreed Joe, and they arranged to meet at two thirty.

'Take these couple of books back to the library for me,' said Dad, as Joe was getting ready to leave.

Joe set off with the books underneath his arm. As he walked down the hill to the library he saw Buggy Donlan and Co. Penny Lawson was tagging along with them. They were arguing among themselves. Joe's first thought was to rush for the sanctuary of the library, but too late — they'd spotted him.

'Look, it's rat trouser Sprattley,' yelled Buggy and the three of them surged towards him. They spread their arms out and formed a barrier.

'The library's for clean folks like us,' taunted Buggy.

'Not for kids like you who play with vermin,' snorted Penny Lawson, and she stuck her tongue out. Buggy made a grab for one of the books Joe was carrying and threw it towards the library door. Joe, in his anger,

barged through the outstretched arms and ran towards it.

'You wait, Sprattley, filthy, dirty Ratley,' called a mocking voice, 'just you wait.'

Joe shot through the library doors, relieved to be out of their way. Donna was waiting inside.

Wilton Library was a modern building with large windows and giant plants standing like sentinels in appropriate places. A tall droopy girl showed them the pet section, but looked blank when they asked for pet rat books. 'She thought we were joking,' said Donna.

'Well, she looked like a rat herself,' whispered Joe, 'with her pointed nose and long flat feet. She was just short of a tail trailing along behind her.' That made them laugh and a frosty-faced old woman told them to shut up. They rummaged around on the shelves but couldn't find a book on rats.

'It's no good,' said Donna, and she

wandered off to look for a ghost story. Joe kept thinking about Teabag and wondering how he was. Suddenly, a large book fell out on to his toes making him jump. *Rodents*, it said on the spine. He fetched Donna and

they squatted down on the carpet behind the green sofa and had a good look.

'Their tails regulate their body heat,' read Joe. 'When they are hot they wear their tails out straight so the cool air can get to them. When they are cold they sit on their tails to keep heat in. You can clean their tails with soap and water.'

'Domestic rats make ideal pets,' read Donna.

They finished the afternoon having a tin of Coke and a packet of crisps in the little snack-bar upstairs.

'Do you reckon Wilfred likes crisps?' said Donna, dipping one into her Coke and watching it go all soggy. It buckled up and reminded Joe of Teabag's trike.

'I wonder how Teabag is,' he said. 'I wish I knew.'

'We'll have to find out somehow,' said Donna, and she went quiet for a moment.

'Snack-bar's closing in five minutes,' grunted the attendant and he started stacking the chairs so no one else could sit down with drinks.

They dawdled down the stairs till Donna jumped the last three, then stood staring at the large display of notices.

'Look,' she pointed. Joe looked. 'What?'

She ran up to the board and pointed at the picture of a rabbit. Up above the rabbit in large letters were the words: PET SHOW – BRIDWORTH, SATURDAY 29 MAY, 2 P.M. Joe looked at her.

'Don't you see?' she said, 'we can take the rats and show them.' Joe felt wobbly inside.

'We can't,' he said.

'Don't be stupid,' she said, ''course we can. It's only two miles away and the bus goes past the Leisure Centre.' Joe sighed. He wasn't really interested in adventure. He just wanted to look after the rats. Donna darted back into the library. Joe couldn't be bothered to follow. He stood watching the photocopier machine thumping and flashing.

Donna was soon back carrying *Rodents* under her arm.

'I've borrowed it,' she said proudly. 'It could be useful.' She didn't say any more about the pet show but Joe knew she would persist with the idea. Donna was that sort of girl! He thought about Teabag again and felt sad. Suddenly he realized he liked the old man a great deal.

Chapter Six

Sunday dragged at Joe's house. Aunt Flo came to tea and he had to wear his best clothes. Joe kept wondering about Teabag.

'Go round,' suggested Mum, 'and see if there's anything we can do to help.' Joe went round twice. Each time the gate swung idly open and no one was there — only the painful remains of the battered trike. The neighbourhood had a lonely feeling; Joe didn't like it. He trudged back home, disappointed.

However, things were certainly lively on Monday evening when they went round. Dick was in the road astride his spluttering bike, revving hard. He handed the keys hastily to Joe.

'Must dash, see you when I get back from the hospital.'

'How is he?' yelled Joe, but he didn't hear the reply as Dick shot off in a burst of noise.

They opened the door of the familiar faded room. Teabag's desk was still cluttered with clock parts and magazines lay higgledy-piggledy on the floor, but the walls sounded friendly. The ticking clocks seemed to go faster and faster to Joe as though pleased to see him. In the corner of the room two little rat faces were pushing at their wire cage. Joe opened their door. Rodney, the brown and white rat, ran straight on to Donna's knee and Wilfred scuttled up Joe and sat on his shoulder, his whiskers gently brushing Joe's ear.

Donna wanted to change their water and top up the seed pot, so Joe amused the rats.

He scrunched up bits of paper and scuttled them on the floor. Wilfred stood still, one paw raised, and listened.

'I shall invent a special whistling sound for you,' Joe told them, 'like this,' and he gave a few high-pitched whistles. Wilfred stopped. Joe quickly gave him a chocolate drop. 'You try it,' he said to Donna.

Donna didn't say anything but her cheeks were going a bright pink and Joe noticed

what a lot of freckles she had on her nose.
She was speckled like a bird's egg.

'Go on,' he urged, whistling until he ran
out of breath.

'I can't whistle,' said Donna flatly.

Joe was amazed. Fancy not being able to
whistle. He tried to show her. They spent
ages practising but it was no good.

'I think I've got the wrong sort of lips,' she
said sadly. At last they put the rats back and
left. 'And don't you dare tell,' flared Donna
as she turned left down Princes Court.

Joe went to visit the rats on his own on
Tuesday as Donna was not at school. Dick
Bailey let him in.

'He's not so bad,' he told Joe quickly.
'Sorry I had to dash yesterday, but it was
nearly the end of visiting time and I'd
promised to go. He's been very lucky,
mainly cuts and bruises from the accident but
they are worried about his cough. I'm just

about to go visit now. Would you like to come and see him?'

'Oh yes,' said Joe.

'It will only be for about ten minutes, mind,' said Dick, as he stuck the red crash helmet on Joe and helped him on to the bike. 'Hang on tightly, Joe. The Cottage Hospital is only down by the park.'

The ward was full of flowers, screens and curtains. A fussy nurse was tucking Teabag's bed-covers tightly in as they arrived. Teabag pulled them all out when she had gone.

'Bah,' he said. 'They try to keep these beds looking as if there's no one in them,' and he heaved his knees up in the middle to ruin the effect. He smiled at Joe. 'I'm not so bad, eh? They say I'll be out in a day or two. They've patched me up nicely.' Apart from a purple bruise on his cheek he appeared to be all right, but he soon looked cross again. 'They say I've to be looked after,' he grumbled.

'They want my sister to look after me or a home help, but Minnie's scared stiff of the rats and I don't want no 'ome 'elp poking 'er nose into my life, and tidying all my clock parts.' He heaved the bed-clothes again and threw out a pillow. Then he started coughing.

'Hold on,' said Dick, as the old man's face got redder and redder. A stiff, starchy nurse bustled over.

'Now, Mr Tetley, settle down. What's this pillow doing on the floor?' She turned to Dick. 'A word, Mr Bailey, please.' She spoke softly out of the corner of her mouth. Dick excused himself and followed her.

'Now, lad, how are the rats?'

'Lovely,' said Joe. He told Teabag about the show and Donna's idea. 'Can we enter them and will you come, Mr Tetley?'

'Love to, lad. Yes, that'll be something to look forward to.' A bell rang noisily to tell everyone it was the end of visiting time. Dick came back.

'Come on, young 'un,' he said to Joe. He tapped Teabag on the arm, 'And you behave yourself.'

'Shall I try and bring Wilfred in to see you, Mr Tetley?'

'Good Lord, no!' said the old man. 'If they saw him, they'd say I needed locking up, never mind looking after. No, Joe, better not bring him, I'll look forward to Saturday.'

They were soon back at number three Summer Street.

'The old boy might end up in a home, Joe,' said Dick, sadly. 'He really doesn't look after himself properly, you know, and gets bronchitis every winter.'

'Bronc what?' said Joe.

'A bad cough, but much worse than the one he's got now. You see, I can't look after him in the holidays, as I go home to my folks for long spells. In fact, I'll soon be going.'

'Perhaps Donna and I could,' offered Joe.

'Perhaps,' said Dick, but he didn't sound too sure.

'I'll just play with the rats a while,' said Joe. He felt in his pocket for the scraps he'd brought them. He made a little tea-party and watched the rats pick out their favourite bits. He wondered if they missed Teabag.

Afterwards Joe stroked them. The animals

closed their eyes with pleasure. Wilfred
climbed on to his shoulder, curled up and
settled down by his neck. Joe thought he had
never felt anything so lovely in his life.

What if Teabag had to get rid of them so
he could live with his sister, or have a home
help? And what if he had to go into a home?
A terrible thought.

Chapter Seven

Wednesday, Donna was back in circulation, all bright and cheeky as usual. 'Had a nose bleed before school,' she told him. Donna could make her nose bleed whenever she wanted by nipping the bridge part. Whenever there was something horrid like a test, Donna's nose would bleed and she would be excused. Joe had tried pinching his nose but it never worked for him.

'Mum made me stay in all day. I read all the rat section in that book,' she told him, 'ready for "Rat Saturday".' She grinned. She'd also spent ages trying to whistle but didn't mention that.

Joe told her about Teabag. At first she looked sulky at having missed the excursion but she cheered up when he told her about Teabag and the show.

'We'll get them all spruced up tonight, ready.' Joe was feeling interested now that Teabag was coming. He agreed to bring along a tea-towel and an old toothbrush and some soap, and Donna said she would bring her mum's casserole dish to bath the rats in.

She was round at Joe's house straight after tea with a heavy-looking schoolbag. They took it in turns to carry it, and had just stopped to change over when they heard footsteps behind. It was Buggy Donlan and his gang.

'You're going to see that old tramp, ain't you?' he scoffed. 'In that rat-infested cellar.'

'No!' said Joe.

They couldn't get rid of Buggy and had to

put up with his torments till they turned up
Teabag's path.

'Liar!' yelled Dominic, and he threw a
handful of gravel at them both.

Donna knocked on the door and hoped
Dick Bailey would be quick and let them in.
Then she noticed a note in the letterbox:
'GONE TO THE HOSPITAL – KEY NEXT
DOOR'. However, Buggy's gang soon

disappeared round the corner.

They let the rats out, then filled the casserole dish with warmish water. Donna popped Rodney in and very gently rubbed her soapy hand over his arched body. He was out immediately, looking soggy and worried. Joe held him in his mother's new tea-towel, the one with cheese recipes on, and gently patted him. Donna reached for her schoolbag and pulled out a hair-drier.

'No, Donna,' protested Joe in alarm.

'Nonsense,' retorted Donna. She plugged it in and held it quite a way from Rodney.

'The book says dry them well. We don't want him getting a chill.' The rat didn't seem to mind at all.

'Now his tail,' said Donna. 'The book says scrub very gently with an old toothbrush to remove dead scales.' It worked a treat. Wilfred had the same beauty treatment. They left them curled up together in their

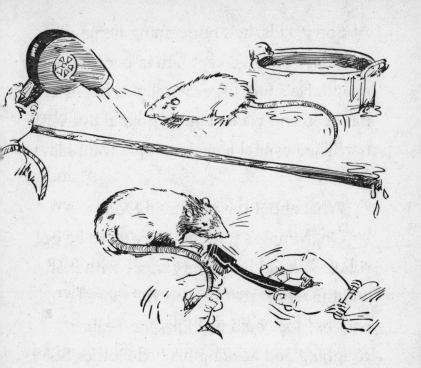

hay-box like two soft woolly pompoms.

'All ready for "Rat Saturday",' said Donna.

The next day, after school, they rushed round to the house to see if Teabag was home. Joe knocked gently at the door and waited. He hoped Teabag would come to the door himself but it was Dick Bailey's quick footsteps that came down the hall. He shook his head slowly.

'Sorry, kids, he's not coming home till Monday. They've kept him in because of his cough. He's furious, especially as his sister has been and wants him to go and live with her. The hospital welfare people want him to go too.'

'What about the rats?' said Donna.

'Oh, Minnie's told him they've to be got rid of. The old boy's very upset with it all and the more cross he gets the more he coughs.' Joe could just imagine Teabag coughing and heaving his bed-clothes around.

When Dick had gone, Joe looked at Donna. 'That's it then, no rat show. What a let-down.'

'How do you mean? We can take them on our own.'

'What if anything happens to them?' said Joe, feeling queasy.

'Such as what?' Joe couldn't think.

'Oh, Joe, you worry too much.' Just what his dad often said to him – 'You worry too much, Joe.' Somehow, Donna sounding like Dad made the whole thing much better. Donna leaned in the doorway, pouting glumly, then straightened.

'Well, I'm going to go anyway, Joe Sprattley, whether you are or not, so meet me here at quarter past ten if you're coming. I'm going home to watch telly,' and before Joe could say anything she'd gone.

Joe bent down and opened the rats' cage. He put Wilfred on his shoulder. The animal curled comfortably round his neck. He reached up and stroked its solid little head with his middle finger.

'You don't mind about the silly show, do you Wilfred?' he said. Wilfred's whiskers twitched on Joe's cheek, in obvious agreement. Teabag couldn't get rid of Wilfred and Rodney. Who would he give them to? I wonder, thought Joe, I wonder if Mum would let me have them. He couldn't get very excited about his wonderings because he thought he knew what she'd say, but still, there was always a chance. He could at least ask.

Chapter Eight

'Come on , Joe.' It was Mum's voice calling up the stairs. 'Pet show day and breakfast's ready.'

Joe got up slowly. He didn't feel like breakfast at all.

'Eat your egg,' fussed Mum.

He stared at the plain lump in his egg cup and wasn't interested.

'Joe, you're not sickening for something, are you?' She went into the other room. Joe cracked his egg. It looked a bit runny. Mum never insisted he ate them if they were undercooked. He trickled one or two drops of milk on the top, ready for when she came back.

'Mum, my egg – look,' he said, showing her the white sloppy egg.

'Oh, leave it, Joe,' she said, 'leave it.'

'Teabag might have to go and live with his sister,' started Joe. 'They say he doesn't look after himself properly.'

'Mr Tetley,' corrected Mum, busy shuffling toast on the grill.

'... and get rid of his rats,' went on Joe. 'I don't suppose I could have them?'

'Now, Joe,' said Mum. Suddenly the toast caught fire. She batted it with a spoon and sent it skidding on to the floor.

'I don't suppose he wants to go to his sister's, Mr Tetley I mean,' she said, bunging the burned offering in the bin.

'No.'

'Hm,' said Mum, 'he's a nice old man. It seems a pity. I wonder ... when is he coming out of hospital?'

'Monday,' said Joe. 'Why?'

greeted her. 'Is he a silver pearl?' she
inquired.

'What?' said Donna.

'Yes, he is,' decided the woman. 'He's a
pearl with a hint of Siamese.' Joe lifted
Rodney out.

'Oh, a cinnamon hooded,' she exclaimed.
'Jedd, come and look at this hooded.' A

young man pushed his way out of a knot of people and came to admire Rodney. He showed Joe and Donna how to enter the rats. There were many breeds being shown: Berkshire, silver fawn, and even a curly-furred rat called a Rex variety. They just got Wilfred and Rodney entered in time. Judging started immediately. Busy assistants carried containers of rats to and from the stage. The judge lifted Rodney out.

'Nice coat,' Donna heard her say. Eventually all the plastic containers had been returned to their places except for four which stood in a row on the judge's table. One of them was Rodney's. The judge looked closely and bit her pencil end. 'We want first, second and third,' she said. She stood awkwardly, one hand on hip, looking hard at them all. Then she shifted position and tapped three cages with her pencil. 'First, second, third.' Rodney's cage wasn't tapped. Joe couldn't believe it. How could anybody not choose Rodney? But they hadn't.

'Never mind,' said Donna, 'he did well to come fourth.' The judge took off her glasses. She seemed less stern now the judging was over.

'He didn't win,' she explained, 'because his hood marking didn't meet underneath his chin. I should enter them both in the "pets class" where they will be judged more for character and condition.'

'Duck' came shuffling over. 'Any luck?' she asked. They told her. 'Right!' She pointed to another table where a man was making notes. 'Go over there, duck, and enter them in "pets class".' 'Duck' – ugh! it made Joe wince, but they did as she suggested.

'Names?' said the man.

'Wilfred and Rodney.'

'No, your name,' snapped the man.

'Joe Sprattley,' said Joe.

'Judging starts at two o'clock,' he mumbled, without looking up.

There was just time to get some food at the snack-bar upstairs. They had to join a long queue. 'We'd better sort out our money,' said Joe, '20p busfare, 15p for a rat badge.'

Going back to the rat judging, they passed the cavies.

'Look,' exclaimed Donna, 'they've got their hair in curlers. The long-haired cavies have their hair rolled up in papers, like Mum on Friday nights before she goes to Bingo!'

'It's barmy,' muttered Joe. The rabbits were nice but rather jumpy. 'Rats are best,' said Joe, firmly. 'Let's go back.' A tall man in a white coat was just coming over to start judging. 'Come on, poppet.' He eased Wilfred out of the cage. Wilfred yawned and stretched, then ran straight up his arm. The judge put him down on the table. Wilfred ran to the edge and peered over. A lady stroked him, so he ran up her arm. Donna nudged Joe as the judge handled Wilfred again. Then he picked up a snowy white rat. Wilfred looked like a dirty tennis ball by comparison. Joe found himself wishing the judge would put it down and pick up Wilfred. The more attention Wilfred got, the more excited Joe became. First the judge held him high up, then turned him round and put him down on the table and straightened out his tail. Finally it happened. 'This one,' said the judge, 'he's so friendly. You're a perfect poppet,' he whispered. Someone stuck a red rosette on Wilfred's cage.

'He's won!' shrieked Donna. 'Duck' appeared. She clapped them on the back.

'Smashing,' she said, 'really smashing.'

Wilfred's cage was moved quickly to another table where a rabbit, a guinea pig, a mouse and a hamster were looking at one another with surprise. There was more talking among the judges.

'Presentation in five minutes,' announced a blaring voice from the stage. Donna and Joe gathered round, along with lots of other people who seemed to be coming from all corners of the hall.

'Ladies and gentlemen, children,' began one of the judges. Someone handed her a silver cup. 'This,' she said, 'is for the Best Pet of the whole show. Our job as judges was very difficult, but we've narrowed it down to three.' Joe felt shaky and Donna got a sudden thirst. Only Wilfred seemed unperturbed. He suddenly managed to nudge off the netting from the top of his cage and climbed out. He hesitated a moment then ran up the judge's coat. Everyone laughed. She stopped her formal speech, smiled and said, 'Well, someone here seems to have jumped the gun.'

Joe had heard that phrase somewhere before. He could remember being told not to 'jump the gun' but wasn't sure what it meant. It didn't seem to make sense.

Then it all happened, while his mind was on guns — 'Silver Pearl Rat — Pet of the Year — Joe Sprattley.' Donna was grabbing his arm. 'Duck' was pushing him forward. People were clapping. A man walked out to the front with a camera pressed to his screwed-up face and before Joe realized it he was out there taking hold of the gleaming silver cup. He felt a familiar weight on his shoulder and a touch of whiskers on his cheek. Flash, went the camera and he heard more cheering.

Suddenly, just as the noise dropped, someone came clumping up to the stage and started to protest. Everyone went very quiet. It was Buggy Donlan.

'It's not his. It's not fair. He should be disqualified!' He pointed to Joe and everyone stared. Joe felt sick. He felt as though the gun Wilfred was said to have jumped was pointing straight at him. The judges looked confused.

'He ain't got no rat,' said Buggy again. '... told you I'd get my own back, Sprattley!' Someone fetched a sheet of paper. 'Cheat,' said Buggy, rudely. Joe had never thought of it that way before but now he did. Of course, it was not his rat and he should never have brought it.

Donna came up and dragged at him. 'Come on, let's go,' she said quietly. 'Leave the cup. Let's get the rats and go.'

'Quiet!' ordered a judge. He raised his glasses and shuffled his papers around. 'The prize goes to the person who has exhibited the animal – not the person who owns it.' He turned to Joe. 'You are Joe Sprattley, are you?'

'Yes,' said Joe.

'Right, don't worry, lad. Someone show that troublemaker the door.'

Buggy scowled and pretended to spit at Joe before he went. As Joe watched him go, he recognized two faces in the crowd – Dobbie Wilson and Jason Tucker. Jason stuck his leg out and Buggy went toppling towards the door. After the prize-giving, Dobbie and Jason rushed towards Joe and Donna.

'Well done, Joe. It's like the football

matches — you don't have to live in a town
to play in their team. Let's have a look at the
cup. Perhaps Mr Priggen will present it to
you in assembly next week.'

'Let's hold one of the rats,' said Jason.

Donna handed them a rat each.

'They're super, aren't they?' said Dobbie.

'Yes, Pet of the Year,' said Joe, pointing
to the words round the shiny cup.

All four went home on the bus together.

Wilfred and Rodney were no trouble this time. They slept in the cage in Donna's bag.

'See you Monday,' called Jason as they parted company.

'A pity Teabag missed it,' said Donna as they put the rats back in their cage. 'I wonder what he'll say. I bet he'll be pleased.'

Joe put the silver cup and red rosette by the side of the cage.

'I hope so,' he said. It had been a terrific day, had 'Rat Saturday', absolutely terrific.

Chapter Ten

Everyone was talking about the Rat Show
when Joe got to school on Monday. Dobbie
Wilson and Jason Tucker were at the centre
of the hubbub. Kids always listened to them.
Joe supposed it was because they were in the
football team.

'Super pets they make,' Jason was saying.
Ryan was already trying to persuade his
sister to have a rat instead of a hamster for
her birthday. They all clamoured round Joe
as he came modestly into the centre. He
didn't have a chance to say much before
Miss Winterbottom came over to sort them
out.

'Miss, Miss, Joe's got a silver cup,' shouted Andrew Doyle. Miss Winterbottom, who was about to use her bossy voice, stopped and listened to the story.

'How exciting, Joe,' she said. 'That's lovely. You must give us a talk on rats and do bring the cup in. I'm sure Mr Priggen would like to see it.'

'Yes,' shouted everyone. Suddenly Joe felt important. It was a nice feeling: one that he didn't often get at school and it lasted all day. Even so, Joe was quite glad when lessons finished and he could go and see if Teabag was home. Donna had to stay at school for her recorder practice but promised to come straight round afterwards.

Teabag opened the door as Joe walked up the path. His face was bright and cheerful and familiar; he did not seem upset at all.

'Come in, lad.' The room ticked its usual welcome – such a lovely room; peaceful,

86

despite the ticking. It was good to see the old man again. He didn't look any different and the purple bruise on his cheek was even smaller.

'You seem to have been away ages,' said Joe.

'Aye,' Teabag wandered over to the mantelpiece where the silver cup proudly gleamed. His eyes twinkled. 'What's all this?'

he said. Joe cleared his throat. 'PET OF THE YEAR BRIDWORTH SHOW 1984,' read Teabag.

'The rats won it,' said Joe. 'Do you mind that we went on our own? They weren't frightened, Wilfred and Rodney ... I mean. They ...'

'Now, steady on,' said the old man. He put an arm round Joe's shoulder. ''Course I don't mind, lad. I'm delighted.' He pointed to the wastepaper basket under his desk. It was tipped over on its side and the rubbish was all around it. Curled up inside were Rodney and Wilfred.

'Now, sit down and tell me all about it.' Old Teabag roared with laughter over the bus bit. 'Now tell me again about bathing them,' he said, when Joe had finished. 'You'll have to give a demonstration.'

'I'm glad you're back,' said Joe. 'You are staying, aren't you?'

88

'Well,' said Teabag, 'you know my sister wants me to go and live with her.' Joe's face sagged. 'She thinks I don't look after myself properly.'

'Oh, but you do,' urged Joe. 'You do, I'm sure.'

'That's what I say. Anyway, I'm not going. You see, I like being on my own. I like to do what I want: ride three-wheel trikes, keep rats, play with my clocks.' Joe nodded; he understood.

'But I thought the hospital said you had to be looked after, Mr Tetley?'

'Ah, well,' smiled Teabag. 'Someone's come up with a terrific idea that suits everyone, especially me, and I hope it will suit you, Joe, because you and Donna are in the plan. Yes, a certain Mrs Sprattley had the idea.'

'Mum?' Joe blinked. 'My mum?'

'Yes,' said Teabag, 'your mum.' He

pointed to a basket of fruit on his desk. 'She's
been round earlier in the day. She's arranged
for me to have Meals on Wheels. That's an
organization that provides cooked midday
meals for old people. They bring it to your
door, and she's organized the women's
group at her church to do my washing once
a week and the shopping in bad weather.
That only leaves the dusting and a few odd
jobs and your dad thought you and Donna
might help. Your dad said it would do you
good.' He winked at Joe. Joe smiled, then
beamed as the full weight of this idea sank in;
no question of Teabag going to his sister's or
into a home; and the rats around all the time.

'Great,' he said. ''Course we'll help.'

Teabag ran his finger along the desk top
and blew the dust off his finger. 'Anyway,
what's a bit of dust around the place?'

'Might make you cough,' said Joe.

'Bah!' said Teabag, 'not it.' The old man

prattled on, delighted with Joe's mum's idea. 'I think Minnie's glad,' he said, 'though there's a lovely clock shop at the end of her road. Last time I stayed with her I nearly got an old carriage clock, but someone offered more money.'

'Oh dear,' said Joe.

'Never mind, ownership's not everything. I enjoyed looking closely at the movement before it went. Which reminds me.' He reached for the cup – 'Yours Joe. Take it, lad.'

'It's really Wilfred's,' said Joe, 'and he lives here.' The old man was quiet a moment.

'Joe,' he began, 'would you like to have … do you think your mother would let you …' his voice trailed away. Joe knew what the old man was trying to say. He looked at Wilfred rolling around in the waste bin. Wilfred would never be allowed to roll around in the waste bin and scatter rubbish in my house, he thought. Wilfred was better off here. No,

he couldn't have a rat of his own and that
was that. But he would be coming here often
now to see Wilfred and Rodney. Teabag was
right. Ownership was not everything.
Teabag was staying. That was the main
point. Things were turning out just fine. He
remembered with a little thrill his Rat Talk to
the class.

'No, Mr Tetley,' he said, 'he's yours.'
Teabag smiled and patted Joe amiably. He
did not pursue the matter.

'By the way, I'm giving a talk about rats at
the school, Mr Tetley. I wonder if you could
bring them and show the class sometime? I'm
sure Miss Winterbottom would like that.'

The old man beamed.

'Love to, lad. I really would,' he said. Joe
hoped Miss Winterbottom wouldn't mind.
He had better tell her what he'd said
tomorrow.

'Listen,' said Teabag. Someone was
coming up the path whistling. The whistling
got louder. Teabag opened the door. It was
Donna, her cheeks bright red and eyes
sparkling.

'I can do it!' she yelled. 'Joe, I can whistle. I
learned in the recorder class. I couldn't blow
a silly high note. Miss Jones told me to go

away and practise for a minute, and suddenly I was whistling.' She giggled. 'I still can't play that stupid note, but I can whistle.' Joe cheered so loudly he startled the rats.

'This calls for a celebration,' cried Teabag. He dashed round and finally produced milk and broken biscuits. The wastepaper basket started rolling and out tumbled Rodney and Wilfred. They ran to Teabag and climbed on

to his knee. Joe told Donna all about his mum's idea.

Teabag listened to their enthusiastic chatter, happily stroking Wilfred.

'Smashing,' said Donna. 'We'll help, won't we, Joe? We'll come as often as you like, Mr Tetley.'

'Good,' said Teabag, 'I'll like that.'

Joe stood up at last. 'We'd better go. Oh, this is for you.' He pulled out a round 'I Love Rats' badge and gave it to Teabag, who smiled happily and pinned it on his old, worn jacket straight away.

'It's true,' he said, smiling, 'I do love 'em.' Donna was already at the door and starting to whistle again.

'Here . . .' He thrust the silver cup into Joe's hand. 'Don't you dare leave this. This really is yours.' Joe took it gratefully.

Donna whistled all the way home. Joe

watched as she skipped happily down her road. She turned and waved. He waved back and hugged the cup to him. He wondered if Mr Priggen really would present it to him in assembly — just like Jason's football cup.